Rule 1:
You can never be completely sure what may happen next.

Ruby Redfort

First published in paperback in Great Britain by
HarperCollins Children's Books 2013

HarperCollins Children's Books is a division of
HarperCollinsPublishers Ltd
77-85 Fulham Palace Road, Hammersmith, London W6 8JB

The HarperCollins Children's Books website is www.harpercollins.co.uk

Visit Lauren Child on the web at
www.rubyredfort.com www.milkmonitor.com

1

Series design and illustrations © David Mackintosh

UK ISBN: 978-0-00-750636-1
Export ISBN: 978-0-00-751231-7
Australian B-format ISBN: 978-0-00-751232-4

Quotes on p.12, 13, 42, 67, 97, 114, and extract on pp.110-1, from *Clarice Bean,
Don't Look Now*; Extract on pp.99-102 from *Clarice Bean Spells Trouble*;
Extract on p.134 from *Utterly Me, Clarice Bean*. Originally published by
Orchard Books. Used with kind permission of David Higham Associates

Printed and bound in the UK by Clays Ltd, St Ives Plc

MIX
Paper from
responsible sources
FSC™ C007454
www.fsc.org

FIRST, AN **IMPORTANT** MESSAGE FROM MY PUBLISHERS...

LISTEN UP BUSTER

RUBY IS NO FOOL, so the survival advice contained in these pages is based on real information. However, it is only to be used in dire circumstances where your safety is at risk, or with adult supervision, because survival involves techniques and tools that, if not followed carefully, can be extremely dangerous. In other words:

● ●

PLEASE DON'T TRY THIS AT HOME.

● ●

HANG IN THERE BOZO

THE RUBY REDFORT

EMERGENCY SURVIVAL GUIDE FOR SOME TRICKY PREDICAMENTS

LAUREN CHILD

HarperCollins *Children's Books*

INSIDE THIS BOOK

7. OK, SO THERE ARE WORSE THINGS THAN BEING LOST

8. DANGEROUS ANIMALS, INCLUDING THE TWO-LEGGED TALKING VARIETY

9. SURVIVAL ETIQUETTE

9½. WHEN ETIQUETTE FAILS: GET ME OUTTA HERE SIGNALS

10. CONCLUSION: NOW YOU KNOW WHAT TO DO WHEN YOUR WORST WORRY COMES YOUR WAY

1.

INTRODUCTION:

WHAT TO DO WHEN YOUR WORST WORRY COMES YOUR WAY

REMEMBER: *Your worst worry is the worry you haven't thought to worry about.*

BASICALLY, LIFE IS ALL ABOUT SURVIVAL – you're dead, you're outta the game buster.

Survival: sometimes life is just that. No time to skip around smelling the roses because you're just too busy gripping onto the cliff edge by your fingernails; you're exhausted and everything in you is telling you to let go. But ninety-nine times out of a hundred it is worth hanging on in there bozo, because, just as things can change for the worse, so too can they get a whole lot more appealing. One minute you're crawling around a desert about to die of thirst, the next you're drinking a glass of ice-cold lemonade, poolside.

The difference between life and death: just a bad roll of the dice?

A calamity can't always be prevented and luck won't always be on your side, but you gotta know luck only plays a part.

. . . .

REMEMBER: *More often than not you can influence how things pan out. Your attitude counts for a lot. NEVER SAY DIE.*

. . . .

This is my **RULE 20: NINETY PER CENT OF SURVIVAL IS ABOUT BELIEVING YOU WILL SURVIVE.**

So long as you keep a cool head then you can make it out of there alive. And, if you make it outta there alive, you have a hope of getting your hands on that glass of ice-cold lemonade. So just keep focused on that, or whatever else it is that gives you a reason to live.

 *For example:*

YOUR BOW-WOW.

YOUR KINDLY OLD GRANDMA.

THAT JELLY DONUT.

THAT EPISODE OF CRAZY COPS YOU'VE BEEN SO LOOKING FORWARD TO.

FOUR REASONS TO LIVE

FOCUS

NO MATTER HOW HOPELESS YOUR SITUATION SEEMS, no matter how tired you are, the thing you gotta do is focus. When in a desperate situation, think about what it is that makes life worth living.

Simple as that: you *have* to live because your dog needs walking or Grandma needs a visit.

Your reward: a jelly donut, an episode of your favourite show. All possible so long as you can dig your way out of that avalanche/navigate your way to land/find water/crawl out of that well/outrun that rhinoceros.

HEY YOU!

REMEMBER:
THE TECHNIQUES AND TOOLS
DESCRIBED IN THIS BOOK ARE
INTENDED FOR EXTREME
SURVIVAL SITUATIONS ONLY
AND MANY ARE DANGEROUS.

↓ ↓ ↓

DO NOT TRY ANY OF THIS AT HOME, BUSTER.

2.

STUFF YOU'LL NEED

RIGHT OFF THE BAT you need to know about some useful things to have on your person when things turn bad. OK, so you won't necessarily carry all these things with you all the time – certainly not if you happen to be a school kid – but if you know you're headed to the wilderness or the back of beyond then here are some survival equipment suggestions.

☛ SURVIVAL TOOLS

It can be super handy to have a mini flashlight with you: I usually keep one clipped to my keyring or my belt loop. Useful not only for illumination, it also can be used for signalling and SOS messages.

Take a **PENCIL** (pencils are better than pens because they don't run out of ink or freeze up in sub-zero conditions).

A **SMALL NOTEBOOK** is good – you never know when you might need to note something down or leave a message for someone else. No pencil? You can make charcoal from burnt wood. Or perhaps you need to leave a message on a slightly bigger scale – depending on the terrain, you might find chalk, flints, sticks or other materials.

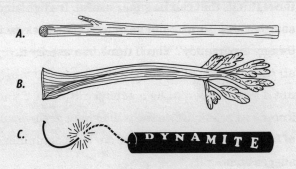

A.

B.

C.

UNSUITABLE STICKS:
A) TOO SMALL   B) TOO VEGETARIAN   C) JUST DON'T, BOZO

Fire is your friend in a survival situation so keep your **MATCHES** safe: don't waste them and don't get 'em wet. A good tip is to keep them in a watertight container at all times.

For obvious reasons a **PENKNIFE** can be very handy in the wild. Use it for gutting fish, cutting up food, string, bandages, whittling wood, and countless other things.

You can use **SAFETY PINS** to remove splinters, replace a missing button or broken zipper, as a fishing hook, to pin a note to a tree, to secure the opening to a makeshift shelter... and I'm sure you'll find a whole bunch of other things to use 'em for.

STRING: what can I say? String is just one of those things that can be super useful. It's light and easy to carry so why not keep it in your backpack for any emergency? You'll think of a use for it.

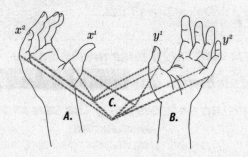

x^2 x^1 y^1 y^2

A.   **C.**   **B.**

I WISH I'D THOUGHT OF THAT

MAGNIFYING GLASS. I'm not gonna dwell on this since I'm sure you all know (but just in case some of you have been living on Mars) you can use a magnifying glass to start a fire. Hold it over some tinder (dry grass and leaves) and let the sun shine through. It will heat up and after a short while make flames. Once you've done that, you can use it to look at tiny things.

. . . .

REMINDER: *In case you're being a duh brain: this method of fire lighting only works if the sun is out.*

. . . .

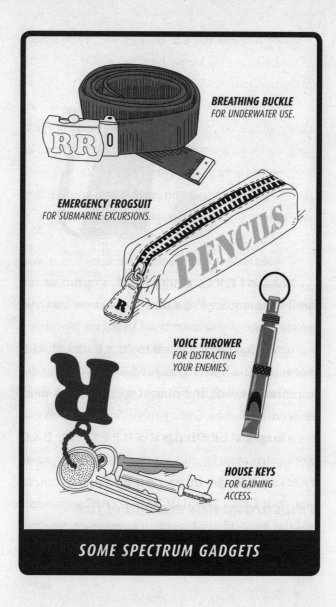

BREATHING BUCKLE
FOR UNDERWATER USE.

EMERGENCY FROGSUIT
FOR SUBMARINE EXCURSIONS.

VOICE THROWER
FOR DISTRACTING
YOUR ENEMIES.

HOUSE KEYS
FOR GAINING
ACCESS.

SOME SPECTRUM GADGETS

Take a **COMPASS** that glows in the dark – but make sure you know how to read it or it'll be worse than useless bozo.

Take **NEEDLES AND THREAD** for fixing clothes, or making an improvised compass if you've forgotten yours.[1] Take a few, and make sure one of them has a very big eye for use with thick threads, or for if you have taken some sinew from a deer to use as thread. You never know, it might happen.

CANDLES are useful for light when you have made shelter. Choose tallow candles, as these are made from fat and can also be eaten in an emergency.

If you can then take a little bit of **SALT** with you; it won't take up much space and salt is an essential nutrient and often very hard to find in the wild.

A large **POLYTHENE SURVIVAL BAG** about two metres by half a metre can be a life-saver. In an emergency you can get inside to preserve heat – but LEAVE YOUR HEAD OUT so you can breathe, bozo. Or, in less of an emergency, you can use it to get water from trees,[2] or cut it to make a sheet shelter.[3]

[1] SEE 'DON'T HAVE A COMPASS', P. 63   [2] SEE 'FINDING WATER', P. 54   [3] SEE 'FINDING SHELTER', P. 51.

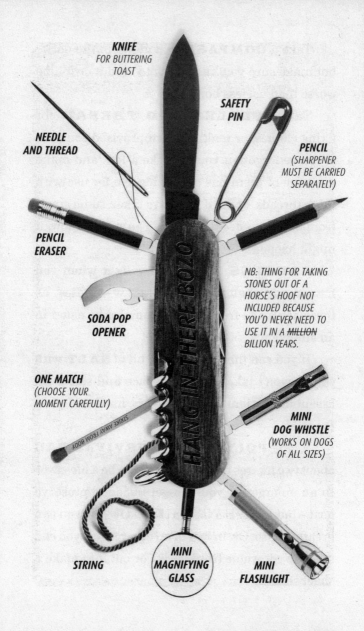

KNIFE
FOR BUTTERING
TOAST

SAFETY PIN

NEEDLE AND THREAD

PENCIL
(SHARPENER MUST BE CARRIED SEPARATELY)

PENCIL ERASER

HANG IN THERE BOZO

NB: THING FOR TAKING STONES OUT OF A HORSE'S HOOF NOT INCLUDED BECAUSE YOU'D NEVER NEED TO USE IT IN A ~~MILLION~~ BILLION YEARS.

SODA POP OPENER

ONE MATCH
(CHOOSE YOUR MOMENT CAREFULLY)

STRIKE AWAY FROM BODY

MINI DOG WHISTLE
(WORKS ON DOGS OF ALL SIZES)

STRING

MINI MAGNIFYING GLASS

MINI FLASHLIGHT

• SAFETY TIPS •

Never carry an open penknife. *When you're not using your penknife, close it and put it away.*

Keep your penknife sharp and dry.
A sharp knife is safer than a dull one because a dull one can slip and cut you.

Make a safety circle: *if anyone else is around then, before you pick up your knife, stretch your arm out and turn in a circle. ONLY if you can't touch another person should you open your knife.*

Never play with knives: *they are tools, not toys.*

Never use a knife to prise something open – *the blade can snap and injure you.*

Only ever pass a knife to another person by the handle, *or preferably with the penknife shut.*

Never hammer the top of a knife to make a hole in something – *the knife can slip and cause injury to you.*

☞ SPECTRUM GADGETS

OK, SO I SHOULD CONFESS HERE that I sometimes get a little helping hand from my spy agency, Spectrum. They supply me with gadgets that have a little more *oomph* than the regular hardware, if you know what I'm saying.

Here are some examples of handy life-savers that have gotten me out of more than one or two scrapes.

THE BREATHING BUCKLE

```
To be used underwater. Slip buckle off
belt, place between teeth and breathe
comfortably for twenty-seven minutes,
two seconds. WARNING! No reserve air
canister.
```

This gadget may be unexciting to look at, but it sure is a life-saver. Take my recent run-in with a giant strangling cephalopod: I would have been deep down ocean-bound, soon to be sleeping with the fishes, if it hadn't been for this little baby.

Ruby raised her gaze one last time. Say goodbye to your world, she told herself, and as she did so, she saw a little silver fish swimming down to escort

her away to the underworld. It twinkled in the
gloom and she looked at it as it moved closer and
closer and became not a fish but a buckle.

The Spectrum breathing buckle... She
snatched it in her hand and placed it between her
teeth. Oxygen filled her lungs.

Air, she thought...

LIMPET LIGHTS

```
Also known as Hansel and Gretel find-
your-way-home glows. Underwater
phosphorescent lights for making a trail.
Guaranteed not to move. Duration five
hours.
```

These work well in an ocean and are especially
useful in rough water since they are tough little
suckers and won't budge for anything... well, not
unless you have the special deactivation removal
device. They are disguised to look like some strange
kind of sea mollusc so, unless you are familiar with
limpet lights, you won't realise they are actually
alien to the seabed.

Ruby had been gone far too long and Clancy was
beginning to flap.

'Darn it Rube, I knew this would happen, I knew it.' He spat these words into the night air as he reluctantly pulled on the wetsuit.

'When I find you, if I find you, I'm gonna explain just how much I hate you, I'm gonna really spell it out in really big letters.'

Clancy Crew had no more respect for any creature on the planet than he did for Ruby Redfort, but right at that exact minute he wasn't lying: he did hate her. He slipped into the black water, all the time praying that the two sea monsters currently at each other's throats (or was it gills?) wouldn't turn their attention on him.

Clancy ducked under the ocean's surface and headed for the islands. Beyond this general direction, it occurred to him that he had no way of knowing what route Ruby had taken or where she had ended up.

Drowned probably, he thought. *Not only am I swimming off on a wild goose chase, but I am gonna have to be grossed out by your dead body.*

He was furious.

But as he swam his attention was caught by small twinkling lights ahead of him: tiny phosphorescent creatures. It was strange how they *were scattered at intervals, almost in a line.*

He followed their trail; where would it lead him?

Of course! he thought. To Ruby!

So limpet lights are pretty smart, but for my money I think ground glows are smarter still.

GROUND GLOWS

To be used when trekking at night in uncertain terrain. Help the trekker retrace his/her steps, or a specified ally to follow the same route. Made up of two parts: pebble-like glow light and discreet shoe fix activator. Instructions: attach activator to footwear and drop pebble glows as you walk. Pebbles will only light when in range of the activator. Multiple activators can be issued.

WARNING: AFTER HEAVY RAINFALL THEY CAN BE ERRATIC AND UNRELIABLE.

These are clever little illuminators because they have the advantage of only being useful to the user. They are very discreet and very handy if you want an agent to follow your trail at a later time without tipping off an enemy tracker. They have aided the rescue of more than a few Spectrum agents over the years.

GETAWAY SHOES

Depress green button on base of left shoe to convert to 'roller shoes'.

If you think these are like those lame wheelie shoes this kid at my school has then you have no idea what kind of outfit Spectrum is.

Depress red button on base of right shoe to activate power jets. Maximum speed ninety-one miles per hour for a distance of seven miles approx. Warning! Can cause feet to overheat. Avoid use on rugged terrain.

I've tried these and all I can say is they are pretty darn cool even when they overheat.

THE VOICE THROWER

This works in the same way as any distraction device by throwing your target off course. It is a highly sophisticated version of throwing a stone to divert attention away from you.

Something in the gadget drawer caught Ruby's eye. It was a silver whistle – looked like a dog whistle but the label was smudged. Maybe it was the ribbon, maybe it was the fact that she had always wanted a silver dog whistle, but Ruby found that she couldn't resist slipping it over her head and looking at her reflection in the glass.

She blew into it – no sound at all. Surely it wasn't just a dog whistle? She blew into it again and again, still nothing. In her frustration she started blowing and inhaling in the way that one might suck air in and out of a harmonica.

'Must be busted,' said Ruby out loud, but her voice seemed to be coming from far, far away. For a second she was puzzled and then it dawned on her: the whistle was no whistle, it was a voice thrower.

She inhaled again. 'Hello,' she said. This time her voice sounded as if it was coming from right behind her. She experimented some more – there were four little holes in the whistle, and whichever one her finger covered determined the direction her voice came from – north, east, south or west of her. Point the whistle up – her voice was thrown above her.

It was precisely at the moment she called out the words, 'I'm over here!' that someone else decided to enter the room.

Ruby quickly ducked down behind the cabinets.

'Did you hear that?' said a voice she didn't recognise.

Ruby froze.

Oh boy, now I'm in trouble.

Now you might think to yourself, a voice thrower, so what? Nice party trick, but how can that be a life-saving gadget? Well buster, it sure as heck saved my life. Take this little situation for example...

Nine Lives Capaldi raised the little gun and pointed it at Hitch.

'Any last words?' she said.

'Let me think,' said Hitch, 'I'm sure I can come up with something.'

Ruby felt for the dog whistle still around her neck.

Nine Lives took aim. 'You better think fast.' Her finger was squeezing the trigger. 'Too bad I'm gonna mess up that nice suit of yours.'

Ruby brought the whistle to her lips and gently inhaled.

'All out of thoughts? Well, I guess it's time to say adios,' laughed Nine Lives. 'Look into my eyes – they'll be the last you see.'

'Not quite!' shouted Ruby. Her voice appeared to be coming from just behind Capaldi, who spun round in confusion – just enough time for Hitch to lunge towards her and grab hold of the diamond revolver...

You see what I'm saying? A split second can buy you a lotta time. Time to flee the scene or, failing that, get stuck into one mother of a fight. Either way you gain the advantage and in a survival-type situation the advantage is what you are looking for.

These are a few Spectrum gadgets I keep about my person – depending on the situation of course, but let's just say you are stuck, for whatever reason, without any of your trusty life-savers, what then?

3.

GETTING YOUR HEAD IN THE GAME

THIS IS WHERE YOUR IMAGINATION COMES INTO ITS OWN. It's when you gotta be resourceful. People have been surviving for thousands of years in harsh environments and tricky predicaments and you can too so long as you make the right decisions.

Homo sapiens is the most adaptable species on the planet, which is why we have risen to the top of the heap and messed things up for most other species. However, if we put this failing aside for a second, we can remember that we truly are survivors by design.

We are survivors because we can...

IMPROVISE.

☞ DECIDE TO STAY CALM

Clancy has a tendency to panic when in a possible life-and-death situation, but he has developed a technique to deal with this temporary loss of nerve. It involves a little bit of method acting – in other words, pretending to be someone else: someone braver. It's not a bad trick if all else fails.

How does it work?

Just pick a person you admire: a superhero, a fictional character, or an expert at whatever it is you happen to be encountering. Darn it, a comedian will do if it helps you to see the funny side – just imagine yourself as someone who might be able to deal with whatever it is *you* are having to deal with, and sort of become them, inhabit their mind.

This technique can be used in all sorts of situations: when one is public speaking, taking a test or exam, or about to face one's biggest fear.

'So Clancy, how did you manage to jump that roof? I thought I had lost you there for sure.'

Ruby was impressed. She was also astonished, and above all she was relieved to see her friend all in one piece. If he hadn't jumped, it was unlikely that he would have survived at the hands of the deadly Baby Face Marshall, but if he hadn't jumped far enough, he would have been dead for sure.

'I just thought to myself, hey, what if I was Ray Max? If I was him, I could jump that roof no trouble.'

Ray Max was a Twinford hero: he was now the best long jumper in the whole state and was no doubt destined to become a world champion. Failure was not in his vocabulary.

Clancy had made it by less than five millimetres: but when jumping a roof, a millimetre or four counts for a lot.

So I'm not saying that pretending to be Ray Max will get you jumping a roof safe and sound, no trouble at all – you could end up splat on the sidewalk, of course you could, but what *I am* saying is that you are *more likely* to make that jump if you have the confidence and belief that you will. Belief is a big part of success.

WARNING FROM THE PUBLISHER:
➤ *don't actually jump off a roof.*

☞ THINK SIDEWAYS

By thinking sideways what I mean is looking at the problem from a different angle. Sometimes what *seems* like the natural, obvious or even ONLY solution is not such a great idea. **RULE 12: ADJUST YOUR THINKING AND YOUR CHANCES IMPROVE.**

Here's an example:

You break down in the desert; you have little in the way of supplies and no one knows where you are. If you stay put, the question is, will anyone find you? Will you slowly die of thirst? Naturally, you want to start moving, to get back to base, to a safe place – why wouldn't you buster? But if you're looking to live, you gotta think again.

Stride off into the desert, and do you even know what direction to head in? Even if you do, how far do you think you're gonna get in this extreme heat, the blistering sun burning down? A few miles maybe, but what good is that when you need to cover a hundred or so to even be halfway home?

No: *think sideways and stay with your vehicle.* It's a shelter from the heat and the cold. It's also a large object in a vast expanse of nothing. It has much more of a chance of being spotted than you do – you will look like an ant to a passing aircraft. Your chances are greater if you just do nothing.

WARNING: *DON'T GET IN YOUR VEHICLE IF YOU'RE IN A DESERT AND IT'S DAYTIME. THE METAL MAY BECOME VERY HOT AND YOU MAY DEHYDRATE.*

DO shelter in the shade BESIDE the vehicle until dusk. Then build a more permanent shelter in the cool to preserve fluids. If your car or plane has crashed, use the wreckage to create your shelter. Oh and keep your trap shut: you'll conserve more moisture with your mouth closed and therefore stand less chance of dehydration.

WARNING: *OFTEN THE THING YOU MOST WANT TO DO IS THE VERY THING THAT IS GOING TO ENSURE YOU WIND UP DEAD.*

☛ BE RESOURCEFUL

If you're missing something that you urgently need, don't whine about it – find a way of getting it.

So you got no matches? Doesn't mean you can't light a fire. Making fire is right up there with man's greatest discoveries. If a Neanderthal can make sparks then surely you can too bozo. (See 'Making a fire', p.45)

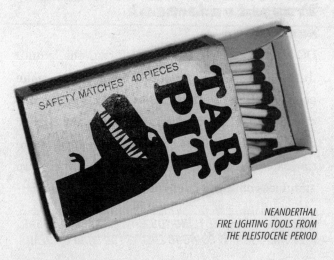

NEANDERTHAL FIRE LIGHTING TOOLS FROM THE PLEISTOCENE PERIOD

Be determined. So you're lost, abandoned, marooned? Big deal: you gotta make it home because what's the alternative? Not making it home, that's what.

You are always hearing about these people who are trapped under car wreckage and somehow manage to get themselves out, lift a boulder, run to hospital with their own severed arm tucked in their jacket, etc. You too can surprise yourself.

Do or die, as Mrs Digby would say. I found myself in just such a tricky predicament not so long ago and here I am to tell the tale.

Trapped underneath something...

Ruby felt herself slipping. She reached out, hoping to catch a branch, a tuft of grass growing out of the rock face, anything, but she was not to be so lucky. Her face, her hands, her knees, all made contact with the mountainside.

*She slid and slid for what to her body felt like an age until, **stop**, she found herself wedged in a narrow crevasse. She tried to move but couldn't:*

*a large rock had dislodged itself and had tumbled
above her to make a badly fitting lid.*

The first thing that occurred to her was: **This
cannot be happening.**

The second thing was: **No one will ever find
me.**

*She was wrong about the first, but quite
correct when it came to the second.*

*She was going to have to get out all on her
own.*

**Let's face it, in this situation your chances of getting
outta there alive are dwindling. No one's coming
looking for you; no one seems to notice that you've
even gone missing. What do you do? Stand there
and blub? Blub all you like bozo, but it ain't gonna**

help get you back to home sweet home (though there are benefits to having a good boo hoo: it can clear the head and alleviate tension, but that's about all).

No, what you gotta do is jump back on your metaphorical horse and get on with the job at hand – surviving.

And that's just what I did when that rock landed on top of me. I got out because I had to get out. I don't know how exactly – all I know is I pushed and pushed against that rock, and even though it musta weighed about a thousand tons, it moved just enough and, with the help of some suntan lotion that I had in my backpack, I managed to sorta squeeze and slide out from under it.

....

REMEMBER: ***The human being is capable of superhuman strength.***

....

4.

SKILLS TO BONE UP ON

IT'S WORTH GENNING UP ON A FEW SURVIVAL SKILLS RIGHT NOW – you never know when you might need them.

RULE 11: LIKE THE BOY SCOUTS SAY, BE PREPARED.

• SAFETY TIPS •

Choose a clear area, at least three metres away from anything that could burn accidentally – trees, bushes, clothing, etc.

———

Ensure there are no overhanging branches – you don't want to set fire to a tree.

———

Never leave your fire unattended.

———

Never leave young children unattended near a fire.

———

Never build a fire in very windy conditions or on an upward slope – fire travels uphill fast because warm air rises.

———

Always make sure to put out your fire completely before leaving it. Even if the flames have stopped burning, the coals may be hot – extinguish the fire with water to be safe, then cover the ashes with earth until the whole thing is completely cold.

☞ MAKING A FIRE

Fires are a must for survival. They can keep you warm, signal your location to passing search parties, allow you to cook food and distil seawater, or even keep bugs away.

Preparation...

You need A FIREPLACE (obviously), TINDER, KINDLING and FUEL.

✳ A FIREPLACE

You're gonna need a fireplace so that you can contain and control the fire.

Clear away all the dry leaves and wood from the immediate area – you're starting a fire, not a forest fire. Make a shallow fire pit and surround with stones.

You wanna find a sheltered place, but make sure it's a ventilated one bozo, where fumes are free to escape. If the ground is marshy or snowy, build the fire on stones or logs covered with earth.

WARNING: DON'T BURN ANYTHING YOU MIGHT NEED... UNLESS, OF COURSE, YOU HAVE TO.

☀ TINDER

Tinder is step one of any good fire. Basically, you wanna find stuff that burns real easily and quickly. Tree bark, dried grass, paper and cotton (from your clothing if you can spare it) make good tinder. Or you could crush up pine cones or birds' nests.

☀ KINDLING

Kindling is step two: this stuff burns a bit slower, letting your largest logs catch and burn. Small twigs make the best kindling. If the outside is damp, shave the twigs with your penknife until you reach the dry part inside.

☀ FUEL

Use only dry wood as your fire is getting going – once it's hot, you may be able to use greener stuff. **Hardwoods** like oak, ash or beech burn well and give off a lotta heat – **softwoods** like pine or bamboo burn faster and give off sparks. But in an emergency buster, you take what you can get!

In the tropics, you may need to shave wood down as everything tends to be damp. In polar regions, engine fuel can be used (for instance, if you have been in a plane crash then you may well have engine fuel at your disposal. Hey, you've got to look on the bright side.) Animal blubber can also burn, if you find a willing seal. And in forested polar places, birch bark and branches burn nicely.

✳ FIRELIGHTING

Make a bed of tinder, then a wigwam of kindling to go around it. Light the tinder. Once the kindling is burning, add larger sticks. Of course, it goes without saying that matches are best for lighting. But what if you don't have a match? At a push you can light fires in other ways. For instance:

✳ DAYTIME: USE THE MAGNIFYING GLASS FROM YOUR KIT

Focus the sun through the lens onto your tinder.

✳ FRICTION

The principle here is simple: get a piece of hardwood and a piece of softwood (see 'Fuel', above) and rub them together to generate heat that will ignite tinder. In practice it's not so simple 'cos it takes about a million years – but hey, at least the exercise will keep you warm till the fire's lit.

1. GATHER SOME TINDER AND MAKE A WIGWAM OF KINDLING STICKS AROUND IT...

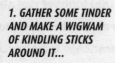

2. LIGHT THE TINDER AND STACK LARGER STICKS ON THE WIGWAM...

3. SOON THE FIRE WILL BE BURNING

CONTINUE TO ADD FIRE WOOD AND BEFORE YOU KNOW IT YOU'LL BE ONE STEP CLOSER TO SURVIVING.

WIGWAM FIRE

> **REMEMBER:** *You're not looking for sparks, you're looking for the wood to start glowing red, so you can use the heat to start a fire.*

THE HAND-DRILL Make a baseboard of hardwood. OK, so this isn't strictly speaking easy. But hey, you're the one who lost the matches. I don't know, look for a fence you can take a board from, or something. Improvise! Use your noodle. (I'm talking about your brain!)

Let's assume you've got your base. If possible, cut a triangular notch in one end to collect your tinder and keep it dry and ready for ignition. Then gouge a little hollow in the board right by the tinder.

Now you need a softwood stick with a sharp end. Put the sharp end in the hollow you just made, and use your palms to spin the stick, pressing down as you do to make as much friction as possible.

Repeat one million times.

When the tip of the stick is red (and you are about to fall over from exhaustion), apply it to the tinder and blow gently.

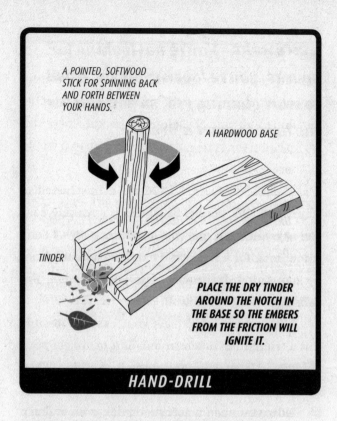

A POINTED, SOFTWOOD STICK FOR SPINNING BACK AND FORTH BETWEEN YOUR HANDS.

A HARDWOOD BASE

TINDER

PLACE THE DRY TINDER AROUND THE NOTCH IN THE BASE SO THE EMBERS FROM THE FRICTION WILL IGNITE IT.

HAND-DRILL

WARNING: THIS METHOD WILL ONLY WORK IN DRY CONDITIONS. EVEN IF YOUR WOOD ISN'T WET, YOU'RE GONNA BE SPINNING THAT STICK FOR A LONG TIME, BELIEVE ME, AND YOU'RE GONNA GET A REAL ACHE IN THE ARM. YOU ALSO NEED SOFTWOOD AND HARDWOOD, WHICH IS A PRETTY BIG ASK IF YOU'RE IN THE DESERT OR STRANDED ON A BEACH. MY ADVICE? DON'T LOSE YOUR MATCHES.

☞ FINDING SHELTER

In pretty much any survival situation, you wanna get out of the wind and the sun as soon as possible and find some kind of shelter. Be careful where you set up camp though: you could wind up in a whole lot more trouble.

WARNING: DO NOT SHELTER: ON TOP OF A HILL, BECAUSE OF EXPOSURE TO WIND; AT THE BOTTOM OF A VALLEY, WHERE COLDER AIR GATHERS; NEXT TO A RIVER THAT IS PRONE TO FLOODING (LOOK FOR HIGH-WATER MARKS); UNDER A WASPS' NEST; NEXT TO A WHOLE PRIDE OF LIONS; ON TOP OF A SLEEPING ELEPHANT. OK, SO THE ELEPHANT'S UNLIKELY, BUT I'M NOT KIDDING ABOUT ANYTHING ELSE. YOU GOTTA KNOW WHAT YOU MIGHT BE SHARING YOUR BED WITH.

Sheet shelter...

A groundsheet or your polythene survival bag can be used to make a bunch of shelters in an emergency. For instance, you can make a triangular shelter with the narrow end pointing towards the wind, the edges weighted down by stones and the 'roof' raised with a stick or, even better, two sticks lashed together. Or you could make a lean-to against a rocky ledge or similar.

TIE THE STICKS TOGETHER

MAKE A PYRAMID OF STICKS AND TIE THE STICK STRUCTURE TOGETHER WITH STRING OR GRASS. DRAPE YOUR SURVIVAL SHEET OVER IT. *

THE ENTRANCE OF THE SHELTER SHOULD POINT AWAY FROM THE WIND

WEIGH DOWN BOTH SIDES OF SHELTER WITH STONES OR DIRT

* IF YOU DON'T HAVE A SURVIVAL SHEET, YOU CAN STACK LEAFY BRANCHES AGAINST THE STRUCTURE TO MAKE WALLS.

SHEET SHELTER

WARNING: USE A SLEEPING BAG OR DRY GRASS FOR THE FLOOR – DO NOT LIE ON COLD GROUND.

If you don't have a sheet: use *anything available*.

RULE 40: IF YOU AIN'T BREATHING, YOU AIN'T SURVIVING.

WARNING: ALL NATURAL SHELTERS WILL HAVE PLACES WHERE AIR CAN GET IN. DO NOT TRY TO COVER THEM ALL. SOME VENTILATION IS ESSENTIAL. YOU GOTTA WORRY ABOUT OXYGEN BEFORE YOU WORRY ABOUT ANYTHING ELSE.

Good places to shelter...

Under a cliff overhang. WARNING: check that the ground is not about to give way underneath you or indeed on top of you.

Natural hollows. Any depression in the ground can protect you from the wind. Make a roof of branches if you can.

Trees. Use large branches that sweep to the ground to shelter under – you can weave small twigs and branches into them to make them more waterproof. Or shelter in the natural overhang under the roots of a fallen-down tree, if it is at the correct angle to the wind. Don't get this wrong, or you'll be shivering in a draught, bozo.

You can also shelter and sleep up a tree. You may consider this a good thing to do if there are wolves or any other non-tree-climbing dangerous animals in the area. Do be sure to secure yourself to a branch or the tree trunk. Tie a scarf or piece of rope round your waist and then round part of the tree. WARNING: DO NOT TIE YOUR LEGS, ARMS OR NECK, BECAUSE IF YOU SLIP FROM YOUR PERCH, YOU MAY END UP AT A GREAT DISADVANTAGE OR EVEN DEAD.

In your own vehicle. Shelter under the wing of your plane or by the side of your car. Make sure you shelter on the side that is out of the wind or you will get pretty cold pretty quick.

☞ FINDING WATER

Water is essential for obvious reasons. Remember the rule of three: generally speaking, you'll survive for three minutes without air, three days without water and three weeks without food. So, unless you find water quick buster, you're not gonna last more than three days.

Animals...

Mammals, birds and insects can all lead you to water if you follow them, as they all need to drink often. Try not to follow lions, tigers and so on, as they will most likely attempt to eat you.

WARNING: DO NOT FOLLOW REPTILES, AS THEY COLLECT WATER FROM THEIR PREY AND SO ARE NOT GOOD INDICATORS OF WATER SOURCES. SO, IF YOU FOLLOW A LIZARD, ALL HE'S GOING TO LEAD YOU TO IS A FLY. ESPECIALLY DON'T FOLLOW CROCODILES. THEY WILL EAT YOU TOO.

Condensation...

Tie the plastic bag from your kit over the leaves on a tree or over ground vegetation, and it will collect condensation for you. Neat, huh?

Solar still...

In a desert and no trees around? Don't panic. Dig a hole in the sand about a metre across and half a metre deep. Place a can in the middle of the hole, then cover it and the hole with a sheet of plastic formed into a downward conical shape. Vapour from the air and soil below will condense on the sheet, then run down it into the can. Hey, I didn't say survival was easy bozo.

Distillation...

Only got seawater? Fill a can with it and put it over a fire. Place a tube in the water and the other end of the tube in a second sealed can. You'll wanna cool the second can, maybe by putting it in some kinda bucket of cold water. That way the vapour coming down the tube from the boiling water will condense in the second can. If you can light a fire *and* do this then way to go buster. You deserve to survive.

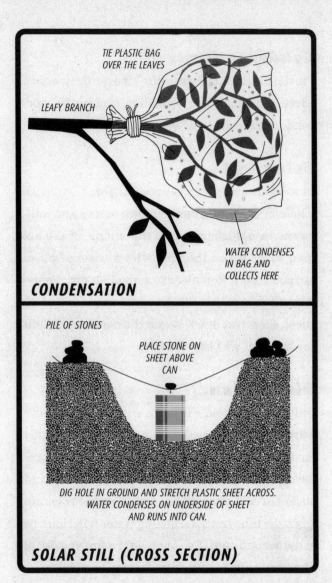

TIE PLASTIC BAG
OVER THE LEAVES

LEAFY BRANCH

WATER CONDENSES
IN BAG AND
COLLECTS HERE

CONDENSATION

PILE OF STONES

PLACE STONE ON
SHEET ABOVE
CAN

DIG HOLE IN GROUND AND STRETCH PLASTIC SHEET ACROSS.
WATER CONDENSES ON UNDERSIDE OF SHEET
AND RUNS INTO CAN.

SOLAR STILL (CROSS SECTION)

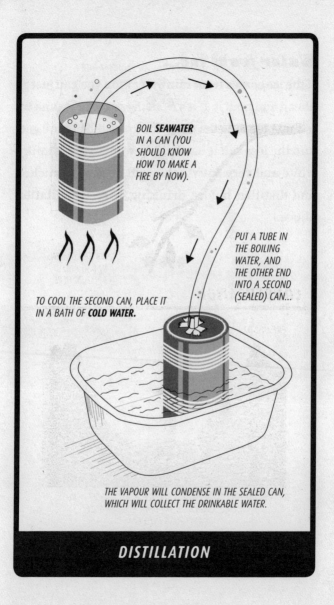

BOIL **SEAWATER** IN A CAN (YOU SHOULD KNOW HOW TO MAKE A FIRE BY NOW).

PUT A TUBE IN THE BOILING WATER, AND THE OTHER END INTO A SECOND (SEALED) CAN...

TO COOL THE SECOND CAN, PLACE IT IN A BATH OF **COLD WATER.**

THE VAPOUR WILL CONDENSE IN THE SEALED CAN, WHICH WILL COLLECT THE DRINKABLE WATER.

DISTILLATION

Water from ice...

If the ice comes from rainwater then you can just go ahead and melt it. If it's from the sea, you wanna try to find blue ice – the older sea ice is, the bluer it gets, and the less salt it has in it. Newer sea ice is milky-white and very salty – this will need to be melted *and* distilled before drinking. (See 'Distillation' above.)

5.

WHATEVER YOU DO, BUSTER, DON'T GET LOST

THE PLANETS AND STARS ARE UP THERE IN THE SKY and able to guide you free of charge to where you got to get. **OK**, so they ain't gonna be able to tell you where the nearest public facility is, but the restroom ain't gonna be top of your priorities for a while – and what the stars *can* do is tell you the general direction to head in.

☞ TRYING TO FIND YOUR WAY IN DAYTIME?

The sun is your friend. The sun is also your compass and your clock. You just gotta remember it rises in the east and sets in the west, and it's at its highest at noon.

☞ IT'S NIGHT AND YOU NEED TO KNOW WHERE TO GO?

Then just thank your lucky stars bozo.

In the northern hemisphere, you wanna look for the North Star – that's in the north, genius. First, find the Plough, otherwise known as the Big Dipper. Then trace a line up the right-hand side of it and you'll find the North Star:

Note how you form a line between, and then beyond, the two stars on the right-hand side of the formation – this will lead you to the North Star.

In the southern hemisphere, you need the Southern Cross, which is found, and you're not gonna believe this, in the south.

WARNING: THERE ARE TWO OTHER CROSS-SHAPED CONSTELLATIONS THAT WON'T TELL YOU ANYTHING USEFUL. YOU'LL KNOW THE SOUTHERN CROSS 'COS IT'S SMALLER, AND HAS TWO 'POINTER STARS' TO ITS RIGHT (SEE DIAGRAM).

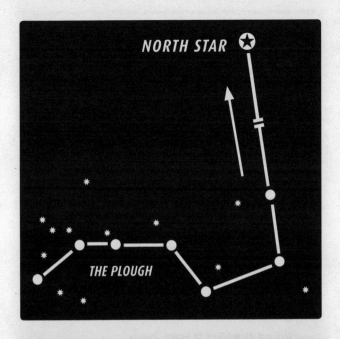

Find the Southern Cross by looking for the Milky Way on a clear night – the band of milky white stars that goes right the way across the sky. In the middle of the Milky Way you're gonna find a little dark patch, and on one side of that dark patch is the Southern Cross, with the pointer stars on the other side.

Once you *have* found the Southern Cross, you just need to know that it's not *exactly* in the south. No, to go due south, you're gonna want to keep the Southern Cross in front of you and just to the left. To be precise about it: take the width of the Southern Cross and count four times that width – then go *that far* to the right of the Cross.

Sound simple? It isn't, bozo.

. . . .

MY ADVICE: *If you're gonna get lost at night, make sure you do it in the northern hemisphere. The North Star is much easier to find. Or, even better, make sure you have a compass.*

. . . .

☞ USE A COMPASS, GENIUS.

What more can I say?

☞ DON'T HAVE A COMPASS?

Don't worry buster – you can make one.

You will need:

> *A needle.*
> *A magnet,*
> *(if you don't have one, you can use silk instead.*
> *OK, I get that silk isn't a whole lot easier to find*
> *in the wild, but what can you do?)*
> *Some thread.*

Stroke the needle repeatedly along the magnet *in one direction only*. This is gonna magnetise the needle. Then hang the needle by the thread – make a loop in the end of the thread for the needle to balance in and swing freely.

WARNING: THE MAGNETISED NEEDLE WILL POINT ALONG THE NORTH-SOUTH AXIS, BUT UNFORTUNATELY BOZO THERE IS NO WAY OF KNOWING WHICH END IS NORTH AND WHICH END IS SOUTH, AS IT DEPENDS ON THE DIRECTION OF MAGNETISATION. LONG STORY SHORT: YOU WANNA USE THIS METHOD, YOU'D BETTER HAVE A ROUGH IDEA OF WHERE NORTH IS ALREADY.

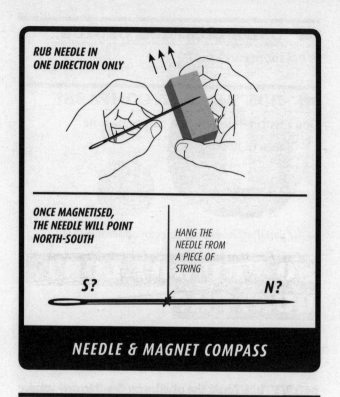

RUB NEEDLE IN
ONE DIRECTION ONLY

ONCE MAGNETISED,
THE NEEDLE WILL POINT
NORTH-SOUTH

HANG THE
NEEDLE FROM
A PIECE OF
STRING

S?

N?

NEEDLE & MAGNET COMPASS

☛ IT'S A CLOUDY NIGHT, YOU DON'T HAVE A COMPASS, AND YOU DON'T HAVE A NEEDLE, THREAD AND MAGNET?

Bad luck buster.

* * *

6.

SO YOU GOT LOST, BUSTER?

THIS IS A PRETTY BAD SITUATION IN SO MANY WAYS. First of all, you don't know where you are; second of all, no one else knows where you are. In other words, you're lost. Being lost can play a lot of tricks on the mind: it's easy to feel hopeless and abandoned, but remember you are not abandoned; you still have yourself and you're gonna make sure you make it out of there. Right bozo?

RULE ONE in a survival situation: **DECIDE ABOVE ALL ELSE THAT YOU ARE GOING TO SURVIVE.**

....

REMEMBER: *People who believe they are going to survive have the odds stacked in their favour.*

....

The first thing to do when you find yourself lost is to not run about like crazy panicking. What you wanna do is remember this four-letter word:

S	*Stand still.*
T	*Take stock of your situation.*
O	*Orientate.*
P	*Plan.*

....

REMEMBER: *Decide to stay calm and don't forget* RULE 19: PANIC WILL FREEZE YOUR BRAIN.

....

☞ WHAT TO DO IF YOU ARE LOST IN THE DESERT

How did you come to be here in the desert in the first place? Well, there are many reasons you could wind up in just such a place – perhaps you got a flat tyre or your camel ran off. Whatever the reason, first thing is you gotta find water.

WARNING: *KEEP YOUR MOUTH CLOSED AS VALUABLE DROPLETS OF MOISTURE WILL EVAPORATE IF YOU DON'T.*

Second, you gotta protect yourself from the sun. Look for shade quickly. You can always make a better shelter once the sun has gone down.

☞ WHAT TO DO IF YOU ARE MAROONED AT SEA

If you are marooned with a group of people then you wanna work as a team. This is true for any survival-type situation, but goes double when stuck in a leaky dinghy miles from shore. Infighting and disorganised thinking are likely to see you dead. If I was stranded in a life raft with Vapona Bugwart, I would try and set aside our differences for the duration of the emergency, or pitch her overboard.

YOU CANNOT AFFORD TO HAVE AN ENEMY SPIRIT ON A LIFE RAFT. An enemy working *with* you, yes; a friend being a massive pain in the butt, NO.

Water is the big issue when marooned at sea so collecting it is your key challenge. If it looks like there might be a heavy squall blowing in, rig up some way of collecting rainwater.

WARNING: *DO NOT DRINK YOUR OWN URINE. IT'S A BASIC RULE AND SOUNDS AN UNLIKELY ONE TO BREAK, BUT AFTER A FEW DAYS AT SEA SUFFERING TERRIBLE DEHYDRATION, YOU MIGHT FIND YOURSELF TEMPTED. URINE IS FULL OF PROTEIN AND YOU NEED A LOT OF WATER TO BREAK IT DOWN AND WATER IS EXACTLY WHAT YOU JUST DON'T HAVE.*

Same goes for seawater.

WARNING: *DO NOT DRINK SEAWATER. THE REASON BEING IT TAKES A GREAT DEAL OF WATER TO FLUSH OUT THE SALT FROM YOUR SYSTEM, MORE WATER THAN YOU GET FROM DRINKING THE SEAWATER IN FACT – I.E. POINTLESS.*

. . . .

REMEMBER: *Someone has to take charge and allocate tasks and chores. Take turns, keep occupied.*

(A) A RAFT ADRIFT

(B) A RIFT

(C) BEREFT

DON'T LET THIS HAPPEN TO YOU

You are more likely to survive a disaster if you keep your mind and body active, and stay calm.

....

☛ **WHAT TO DO IF YOU ARE ALONE IN THE WILDERNESS AND HAVE NO CLUE WHERE YOU ARE**

The boat was a total wreck and Ruby had been lucky to make it to shore at all. 'I'm here,' she had groaned as she'd crawled out of the water, her sodden sweater weighing her down, her waterlogged sneakers oozing icy cold.

But where was here exactly? She hadn't the faintest clue, but right now this wasn't at the forefront of her mind: surviving the night was.

First off buster: You need to think clearly and leave the panicking to people who don't know any better. Don't worry too much about where you are. Worry about surviving. This is where the STOP rule comes in. Stand still. Orientate. Take stock of your surroundings. Make a **plan**.

Sometimes, of course, things turn against you.

*Ruby could see from the dark clouds that there
was a storm brewing and, just to emphasise this
nasty reality, in the distance she heard the rumble
of thunder.*

*Her clothes were already sodden from the
swim – it wasn't like they could get any wetter –
but the prospect of getting soaked all over again in
a freezing downpour did nothing to lift her spirits.
She had saved herself the trouble of drowning only
to die of hypothermia.*

**In this rainy situation keeping warm is key and,
if you're gonna keep warm, you need to dry off so
you'll need shelter and a fire.**

**OK, so it's one thing gathering fuel, another
lighting it with wet matches, and something else
altogether to try and keep it all alight when you're
about to get rained on by a serious cloud. But you've
gotta try – you've gotta decide to survive.**

So basically you've gotta improvise.

*Ruby dragged what was left of her boat out of the
water and across the shingle beach. The wood was*

far too wet to burn, but the bow of the boat would serve as a shelter so long as she faced it out of the wind's cruel bite.

But first she needed to get dry and warm. She shed her soaking knitwear; it would take an age to dry out and she would die of exposure before that happened. It was hard work finding and gathering the necessary fuel, but that was no bad thing: it helped her keep warm; it helped her focus. She had chosen a spot out of the wind underneath a small natural overhang reasonably sheltered from the inevitable rain.

Once the fire was made and alight, she then began gathering branches, pushing them into the ground around the upturned boat wreck. Then, using her penknife, she cut some fir tree branches and tied them to her existing framework. Before long she had made a makeshift shelter, reasonably dry and fairly windproof. It wasn't going to be a pleasant night, but she would at least wake to welcome the dawn.

7.

OK, SO THERE ARE WORSE THINGS THAN BEING LOST

EVEN WHEN YOU KNOW EXACTLY WHERE YOU ARE, you can get into a whole lot of trouble. Here's what to do if you find yourself on the wrong side of Lady Luck.

☞ HOW TO SURVIVE QUICKSAND

WARNING: *DON'T STRUGGLE: IT WILL ONLY MAKE YOU SINK FASTER.*

The first thing you gotta know about quicksand is that, contrary to what old movies say, you will not sink further than your waist *so long* as you don't start flapping about. If you do then things will get more serious as you displace the water and make the sand denser, and so make it that much harder for you to get your feet free.

. . . .

REMEMBER: *You are not gonna drown in quicksand, buster. No, you are much more likely to die of thirst or exposure. If you know someone's gonna be along shortly to pull you out of there then relax, but if not then you better get on with rescuing yourself.*

. . . .

What you gotta do is lie back and allow yourself to float – the human body is less dense than quicksand so floats easily. The more of your body that lies on top of the water, the better chance you have of freeing your feet.

Think slow motion...

The key to freeing yourself is to move very slowly and very gently. Make small circular movements with your feet. No sudden freak-outs. Your aim is to gradually get your whole body to float. Then make tiny circular movements with your hands and paddle yourself to the edge where you can hopefully grab onto something and slither out.

When walking in an area where there is likely to be quicksand, carry a long strong stick. Use it to feel your way. If you fall into quicksand then it can also be used to free you.

....

REMEMBER: *A lot of survival advice means going against human instinct: which makes you wonder what we have these instincts for.*

....

☛ HOW TO SURVIVE A FOREST FIRE

Where's the fire?...

The first clue might just be a plume of smoke in the distance – it might seem like a long way away, but that can change pretty quick. Once you see ash and embers raining down, it could be too late.

If you can get outta there before the fire moves your way then this should be your first course of action. Don't hang around taking in the spectacle – fire travels fast and a change in the wind can mean it's headed in your direction.

IF THE STICK YOU'RE USING TO SEND A MESSAGE LOOKS SIMILAR TO THAT PICTURED BELOW, **DON'T HANG AROUND...** IT COULD BE TOO LATE.

SUREFIRE DANGER SIGN

Facts...

Forest fires travel uphill faster than they travel downhill.

Forest fires move faster depending on the strength of the wind. You obviously want to move in the opposite direction to the fire, but if you find yourself on the wrong side of it – i.e. it's coming towards you – this is easier said than done.

....

REMEMBER: *Don't panic! STOP. Stand still. Look around you and assess the situation.*

....

What you're looking for is a natural firebreak: this might be a road, a river, a lake or a rocky area with not much vegetation. If you're lucky enough to find such a spot, put this area between you and the fire.

Mission accomplished?

NO, whatever you do, keep moving bozo: this is not the time to breathe a sigh of relief. If you do, you're likely to get a lungful of smoke – you are not outta the woods yet. Keep on moving away from the blaze as fast as you can. A firebreak might slow the fire down, but it won't necessarily stop it dead.

What to do if you're all outta luck...

No firebreak in sight? Well, your instinct will quite naturally be to run because who wants to hang around getting burnt to a crisp? But unless you can be sure to run at a steady fourteen miles an hour you wanna think of a better plan.

....

REMEMBER: *THINK SIDEWAYS.*

....

What you can do is make your own firebreak by fighting fire with fire.

So the forest fire is travelling towards you and there's no way out... this is what you do, and it might seem crazy: *set fire to the scrub behind you.*

WARNING: *DO NOT LIGHT A FIRE IN FRONT OF YOU (UPWIND OF YOU) BECAUSE IT WILL BE MOVING TOWARDS YOU AND YOU WILL FIND YOURSELF TRAPPED AND IN A WORSE STATE THAN THE ONE YOU WERE ALREADY IN.*

No, instead, light your fire *downwind* of you so that it travels away from you in the direction of the wind. Once the fire you have set has moved on, you can then run into this burnt-out area. By the time the main forest fire reaches you, it will have nothing to burn and you should be safe inside your firebreak.

....

REMEMBER: *The ground underfoot may be very hot.*

....

WARNING: ONLY TAKE THIS VERY DANGEROUS COURSE OF ACTION IF YOU ARE ABSOLUTELY DESPERATE OR YOU REALLY KNOW WHAT YOU ARE DOING. IT IS A LAST RESORT.

Another last resort...

This is what you should do: get low, because heat rises. Find a ditch or, failing that, dig a trench no matter how shallow and lie face down on the forest floor. Cover your coat in earth and then pull the earth-covered coat over you, trying not to leave any bare skin exposed. Then wait for the fire to pass. If you're lucky, the earth both under and over you will protect you from the heat and the flames.

It goes without saying that if there's water around then submerge yourself in it rather than chancing the method above.

☞ HOW TO SURVIVE A RIP CURRENT

Suddenly Ruby's surfboard was snatched from under her and she was flipped up, flung backwards and tumbled inside the same giant turquoise wave that moments earlier had been carrying her so skilfully to shore.

She felt its tremendous power as it swirled her down into the ocean, her body tugged towards the seabed and her limbs wrenched in all directions. The noise pounding in her six-year-old ears was disorientating: she couldn't see, she couldn't breathe, she was drowning.

Then the wave released her, pushed her back through the water, and she was returned to her own element, spluttering and gasping for air. She glanced around for her board, but it was way off in the distance being tumbled and tossed by the breakers. She struck out for shore, but with every stroke she took she found herself further from land.

She was caught in a rip current.

This was a tricky situation because I was so young and at that time not very strong, but luckily I

ESCAPE ESCAPE

ESCAPE ESCAPE

RIP CURRENT

BEACH

HOW TO ESCAPE A RIP CURRENT:
STAY CALM AND DON'T TRY TO
BEAT IT, BUSTER

had read about these kinds of currents in my encyclopaedia. People sometimes call them rip tides, but they don't have anything to do with the tide: they're usually formed at a break in the sandbar beneath the water, when waves coming towards the beach are forced back, through the break, out to sea.

Contrary to popular belief, they don't pull you under either – they just pull you out with them.

Rip currents are still dangerous though because they want to carry you off out to sea and your natural urge is to resist this by swimming against them. You will never win. If you continue to fight the current, you will tire and eventually (without rescue) you'll be fish food buster.

Here's what you gotta do: crazy as it may seem, relax and let the current take you out as far as it's going to (probably a hundred metres or so) and, once it has released you, swim parallel to the beach until you are past the current's grip and then head for shore. Rip tides are usually only a metre or so wide, though remember that they can be much wider – up to a hundred metres sometimes.

If you have a little more experience and strength then you don't need to wait for the current to stop pulling you: instead, swim parallel to the shoreline. You will find you are still carried out to sea, but will reach the current's edge more quickly – again, once you no longer feel the current's pull, you can start heading into shore.

> 'I saw you waving Ruby honey,' said her aunt, adjusting her large white sunglasses. 'You looked like you were having a wonderful time, though I don't like you swimming so far from shore. I think there are rip tides out there.'
>
> 'No kidding,' said Ruby, sinking to the ground.

8.

DANGEROUS ANIMALS, INCLUDING THE TWO-LEGGED TALKING VARIETY

THERE ARE A WHOLE LOTTA CREATURES you wanna avoid in any survival situation, for the obvious reason that they would like to eat you or kill you – or even just bite you a little, which let's face it is never a whole load of fun.

Rattlenakes...

....

ADVICE: *Never step on a rattlesnake.*

....

Rattlesnakes are found in various parts of the United States, Canada and Mexico. You find them pretty much everywhere in Central and South America: anywhere that is wilderness.

When walking in snakish environments, tread carefully. You are not their prey, but they will strike if they feel threatened. Let them know you're coming and give them the chance to disappear. Avoid reaching under rocks: snakes hide under rocks and in dark hollows to get out of the sun. Always check your footwear before sticking your toes in, likewise sleeping gear.

If you spot a snake on your travels you might be interested to know: is it life-threatening? What type of reptile is it? My advice: don't get too close. *Better to assume all snakes are dangerous than the other way around*.

If bitten by a snake, you need to get hold of some anti-venom pretty darned quick: not easy in the wilderness.

You will also need to identify the snake because you need to know what venom you're dealing with; take the wrong anti-venom and it's curtains my friend.

✳ HOW TO SPOT A RATTLER

Rattlesnakes are pit vipers, not because they live in pits but because they have *a small depression (the pit) between the eye and nostril*. These are heat sensors, used for detecting prey.

Like most venomous snakes, they have a *flat triangular head*, shaped this way for storing venom.

But the big clue is the *rattle on the end of the*

tail. They use this to warn their enemies to back off, so if you hear it rattle, be warned.

✴ DEALING WITH THE BITE

Make sure you don't get bitten again, *so move away from the snake.*

Stay calm, *DO NOT RUN AROUND; this will make the poison spread quicker.*

Remove constrictive clothing and watches, rings, etc. – *you are probably gonna puff up like a balloon. DO NOT apply a tourniquet.*

Wash the puncture holes with water.

If you have a snake-bite kit handy then suction the wound; if you don't then DO NOT USE YOUR MOUTH to suck out the venom.

Keep the wound lower than your heart and if bitten on the arm then make a sling.

Get medical assistance.

How to charm a snake...

Don't even go there buster.

What some people say about snake charming: the snake isn't so much charmed as confused. And a confused snake is an unpredictable snake.

Confuse 'em. Defuse 'em. Unlike with snakes you are actually charming this poisonous personality. Confusing them by being nice. **Killing 'em with kindness.**

Find their weak spot...

Mrs Bexenheath, she's the secretary at Twinford Junior High and she can be one tricky customer: sometimes she's all smiles and nice words and other times she's a real viper. She can even come across as pretty stupid; this is because she sorta IS pretty stupid (that sounds harsh I know, but it's accurate). Anyway, what I'm saying is: just because a person ain't the sharpest knife in the drawer doesn't mean they ain't capable of causing you a whole lot of pain. If they're tricky, like Mrs Bexenheath is, then they need careful handling.

Mrs Bexenheath, the school secretary, looked up to see what at first glance she imagined must be some Hollywood film star. It was as if he had unwittingly strayed off the 'walk of fame' and wandered into the shabby halls of Twinford Junior High – so entirely out of place was he.

However, this handsome man struck up an easy conversation with her and before a minute had passed Mrs Bexenheath had found herself agreeing to excuse Ruby Redfort from all lessons for the foreseeable future. She had concentrated carefully, all the while staring into his Hollywood eyes, wondering were they brown or were they hazel. And, although after he had left she couldn't exactly remember why she had excused Ruby from classes, she did find herself very sympathetic.

'Of course! Of course, she must take all the time she needs,' she had gushed.

'Just remember, Mrs Bexenheath, keep it hush hush – oh and don't bother Mr and Mrs Redfort, if you need to ask anything then be sure to bother me.'

'Oh, I will, I will,' said Mrs Bexenheath sincerely.

Hitch thanked the school secretary for her warmth and kind-heartedness, and promised that yes, he would make a point of visiting the school again soon. Then he said goodbye and returned to the car where Ruby was waiting.

'So?' said Ruby when Hitch got back into the driver's seat.

*'Mrs Bexenheath passed on her warmest
wishes and insists you take all the time you need.'
'Really? What did you tell the old crab apple?'
asked Ruby.*

Ignore...

There are exceptions to the killing with kindness
rule and Wendall Levitt is one of them.

Mr Levitt is himself a contender for Grinch of
the Year and should be avoided at all times; though
as with rattlesnakes this is not always possible. He
happens to run the local pet store: I totally avoid
entering the premises, but sometimes Bug ambles
in looking for dog biscuits. Mr Levitt is no animal
lover – he loves people even less.

For old Mr Levitt it wouldn't matter if he woke
up to find he had won the lottery, he would still
feel he had been short-changed. Spend fifty cents:
you're wasting his time. Spend fifty dollars: now he
has to spend time restocking the shelves in his store.

What to do if your husky wanders into a pet store owned by a Snakish Individual who thinks he is being Reasonable...

Ruby watched as her dog, Bug, ambled into Mr Levitt's store. She winced, knowing that there was no way the husky was going to come out of there without her going in after him.

Over the years, she had watched Mrs Digby dealing with the problem unsuccessfully and getting into one scrap after another. Mrs Digby's problem was that she was not prepared to put up with the old man's complaints and arguments and general blaming of everyone else. **Fair enough**, thought Ruby, but the downside was that Mrs Digby would always come out fuming and battle-weary.

Ruby had adopted a better method. What she had figured out was that there is no point getting into an argument with someone who knows they are right – even if you know that they are not.

You are best to totally ignore this person. You will never make them see the light, and you will die trying. (See 'How to survive a Rip Current', page 81.) They will never, ever like you because, let's be straight here: they don't like anyone and this ain't gonna change, not in a million.

Ignore, ignore, ignore.

A last word on snakes...

So long as you don't come into contact with their fangs, snakes are pretty harmless... well, except for anacondas and pythons and the strangling or swallowing types.

Anacondas...

The anaconda is a huge animal-swallowing snake, often in excess of five metres long and capable of opening its jaws incredibly wide to digest an entire goat, deer or caiman (South American crocodile) without taking one bite.

So there you are in the Amazon rainforest, just tucking in for the night, when you realise it isn't your sleeping bag you're snuggling into, but a giant anaconda. What do you do?

First of all, don't struggle; it won't get you anywhere and you'll just waste valuable energy.

What you should do is stay calm (yeah, right) then slowly reach for your handy penknife which you should keep attached to your belt for just such an emergency. Pull it close to your chest and hold it in both hands. Now wait. That's the hard part; you gotta wait until you're all but swallowed up in the snake's body. Once your arms are inside, point the

THIS IS HOW TO DO IT:

1. DON'T STRUGGLE.   2. STAY CALM.   3. WAIT FOR THE RIGHT MOMENT...

YOU'VE LEFT IT TOO LATE IF...

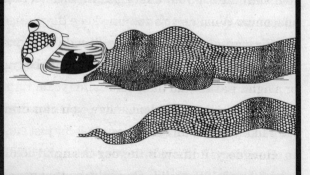

REMEMBER: THERE AIN'T NO ZIPPER ON AN ANACONDA.

knife straight up and stab the snake through the head: this will kill it. You can then pull yourself free and climb out unharmed.

Don't be surprised if you feel a little bit wobbly after this encounter – it's perfectly natural.

☛ HOW TO SIDESTEP AN ANGRY DOG

So you're walking back from the store happily stuffing candy into your mouth when you're confronted by an angry dog.

Angry dogs are dangerous dogs.

Never look an angry dog in the eye. Never turn your back on an angry dog and for jeepers sake never run away. You wanna keep the animal in your sights without looking directly at it and without showing you're either scared stupid or up for a fight. Easier said than done.

Try and look confident – hey, you can even yawn like you couldn't care less.

How do you know if the dog is angry? Well, check its tail. If the tail is standing up, that pooch might just be furious. If it's low and moving from side to side, you're probably OK.

Now take a peek at Fido's mouth. Are his lips back, his teeth bared and his ears forward?

Bad sign.

Ears back? This is a little better: chances are he's scared and ready to protect himself, but won't just attack you for no reason.

You're pretty sure the dog IS angry? OK, try these tips:

> **Lick your lips.** *Dogs send calming signals to other dogs by licking their noses – now you know this, you will notice it all the time! If you can lick your lips really obviously, it will show that you're not a threat.*
>
> **Yawn.** *I wasn't kidding about this. A person or a dog who is yawning is not a person or a dog who is spoiling for a fight – so it will send a signal that you're not aggressive. And possibly that you're sleepy.*
>
> **Back away,** *without looking the dog in the eye.*
>
> **Best of all: back away while yawning and licking your lips.** *I'm serious here buster.*

In many ways dealing with an angry individual is very like dealing with an angry dog. So the same basic advice applies to managing this particular situation.

☞ HOW TO SIDESTEP AN ANGRY INDIVIDUAL

First off, if at all possible, avoid them! Sometimes this is not so easy since angry people are often spoiling for a fight. If the avoidance method is not available to you: let 'em talk – just make soothing noises and calming gestures.

WARNING: DO NOT TRY AND ARGUE WITH THEM: EVEN REASONING CAN BE RISKY IF THEY ARE VERY MAD.

Work hard to appear like you're interested in their ranting and are really taking on board their grievances and general tiresome moaning.

Be careful not to sound patronising or afraid: this only makes a mad person madder; it's an indication to them that they are coming across as unreasonable and this infuriates them further.

WARNING: DO NOT LOOK LIKE YOU'RE TRYING TO GET OUTTA THERE AS FAST AS POSSIBLE.

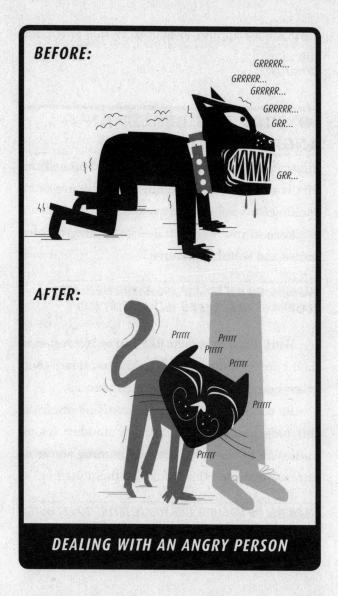

DEALING WITH AN ANGRY PERSON

ADVICE: *Get outta there as fast as possible.*

Mr Parker, our neighbour, is a very angry person and even a friendly hello can put a crimp in his day. My dad always says, 'Wave and walk on by.' Pretty good advice coming from the world's friendliest man.

Sometimes, though, you just can't avoid a confrontation with such an individual. In that case, my advice is: lie like crazy.

Vapona Bugwart had got a hold of Clancy Crew's math book; she was throwing it up in the air to her sidekick the nasty Gemma Melamare. They were enjoying themselves until they saw the school bus coming.

'Gotta split,' sneered Vapona, then tossed the book as high as she could and flung it right over Mr Parker's fence.

Clancy stood motionless.

'Oh brother!' he moaned. The last thing he felt like doing was coming face to face with Mr Parker, but on the other hand the very last thing he felt

like doing was explaining to his dad how he hadn't been able to do his math homework because some girl had thrown it into some guy's yard.

He took a deep breath and scaled the fence adjoining Mr Parker's house: it was a brave move, but the thing was he could see his math book lying there in the midst of Mr Parker's roses, and there was no sign of Mr Parker himself. The coast was clear: if he was quick, no one would see.

However, just as Clancy reached the rose bed, he felt a nasty tug to his ear.

'What are you doing in my yard sonny?' Mr Parker was beside himself; he looked just about ready to call the cops. Clancy was in a lot of pain and all out of explanations. Lucky for him that's when Ruby Redfort showed up.

'Did you catch it Clance?' she wheezed, as if she had been running.

Clancy stared at her. He had no idea what she was talking about. 'Uh... umm?' he said.

Clancy was looking at Ruby out of the corner of his eye, trying to catch her drift; his ear was still being tightly held by Mr Parker.

MR PARKER: 'Catch what? What are you kids up to?'

RUBY: *'Oh, hi there Mr Parker.' Ruby was looking around her, concerned but confident. 'You see,' she continued, her palms upturned in a sort of "trust me" gesture, 'Clancy saw a giant rodent run into your rose bushes; my father says they play havoc with roses and are always chewing up his and just give 'em two seconds and, well, you can forget about winning that best-in-show rose award if you know what I'm saying. Thank goodness Clancy was there; he practically flew over your fence when he saw it, didn't you Clance?'*

CLANCY: *'...Yeah? ... Oh... uh huh.'*

RUBY: *'Clance just hates those giant rodents, don't you Clance?'*

CLANCY: *'Hate 'em.'*

RUBY: *'Clance is a real rose appreciator.'*

Mr Parker let go of Clancy's ear and cocked his head to one side as if he was considering what Ruby had said. Clancy backed away slowly and, while Ruby continued to make calming conversation, he retrieved his book. Mr Parker had his eyes fixed on Ruby and didn't see. Ruby's eyes were looking towards the house, away from Clancy; she looked casual, relaxed.

'My dad uses rodent wire to prevent the critters getting anywhere near his roses, but when you have roses as fantastical as yours, I imagine even rodent wire doesn't keep 'em away.'

Mr Parker looked pleased: he liked the idea of rodents being attracted to his roses.

CLANCY: 'I'm afraid I didn't catch it. I think it went into the Smithersons' yard. I better go and warn them.'

Mr Parker disliked the Smithersons even more than he disliked school kids so he couldn't help looking pleased about this.

Ruby yawned. 'We better get going now Mr Parker.' She walked in a loop around him and he watched them go; he just stood there unsure what he should think, the anger gone, and then he sat back down on his deckchair a tad bewildered.

☛ WOLVES

Ruby and Clancy had been trekking for several hours; the moon was full and casting an eerie glow over the craggy mountain tops. The clouds dragged slowly across the sky and, apart from the sliding of loose stones underfoot, the night was quiet.

Neither of them spoke as they made their way quickly but carefully down the rocky escarpment; they didn't speak a word until they entered the dense pine forest that circled the mountain's edge. The trees stood tall and straight and perfectly still.

They came to a stop and looked around them. The silence was broken by a howl that echoed through the forest and reached far into the night.

'Did you hear that?' said Clancy, his voice full of alarm.

'Wolves,' said Ruby.

'Wolves? Did you say wolves?' said Clancy. 'I have a thing about wolves.'

'You have a thing about most things,' replied Ruby, marching ahead.

'I know but I have a particular thing about wolves,' he continued.

'Oh yeah, and what particular thing is that?' said Ruby.

'I particularly don't like them,' said Clancy.

'I expect they feel the same way about you,' said Ruby.

'But they aren't scared of me,' shivered Clancy.

'Yeah, well, I wouldn't let on if I were you; wolves are good at identifying the weak and vulnerable.'

'Now I'm really scared,' said Clancy, looking into the dark forest. 'People always identify me as weak and vulnerable.'

'Clance, wolves don't usually attack humans... well, not unless the wolves in question have rabies.'

'Is that meant to help?' said Clancy, looking at her in disbelief.

'It's highly unlikely they have the disease, not here,' Ruby reassured him. 'No, these ones are more likely to attack because they see kids, particularly scared kids, as an easy meal ticket.'

BE PREPARED

Clancy turned to look at Ruby. 'Are you for real?'

'I'm just saying,' she shrugged. 'I'm not trying to freak you out.'

'Well, FYI, I am freaked out, **OK!**' said Clancy.

If there is likely to be an encounter with wolves...

Make a fire (remember to follow the correct fire-safety procedure).

Climb a tree (you can sleep up it – see 'Finding Shelter', page 51).

Look strong but unthreatening.

Wolves are pack animals: there is always a leader and the pack does what the leader says. Wolves are looking for easy prey so don't appear vulnerable and don't come across as scared.

☞ OCEAN PREDATORS

Ruby started to make for the ocean surface. And then she caught her breath. Menacing grey shapes, like circling planes above her.

Sharks.

They were between her and the boat; they were between her and the boat and her and the rest of the ocean; they were everywhere, surrounding her, circling like some bullying mob.

But one of them wasn't circling; one of them
was moving towards her...

OK, so you meet that shark you've been so eager to run into ever since you saw the film about the man-eating great white monster chomping on the surf-loving public.

What do you do?

As with so many of these situations, it's best to go against instinct and act bold and brave rather than flapping your arms and peeing yourself.

If you are under the water...

Stay still. If it comes towards you then swim towards it.

Sharks spend most of their time looking for something good to chow down on and they are not known for their good eyesight. What they aren't looking for is a fight so, by swimming toward them, you are letting them know that you do not consider yourself dinner.

If your shark friend doesn't take the hint then poke it with a stick. If you don't have a stick then bop it on the nose with the flat of your palm.

FACT: *Sharks have very sensitive schnozzes.*

DON'T BE FISH FOOD

If you are swimming above the surface and you spot a shark...

Do not thrash around and for jeepers sake do not start peeing yourself.

Fight back: sharks can't be bothered to take on an angry swimmer if there's something a bit tastier out there like a nice blubbery seal. Put your head underwater and shout; sharks don't like a commotion. Swim with firm, strong strokes – don't flap about like you're scared stupid; they might mistake you for an injured fish.

If they do take a bite, they're more than likely not gonna take another: human flesh is not their thing, but this doesn't make a whole lotta difference as to whether you bleed to death or not. The good news is that the cold of the water will mask the agony of the bite and most victims claim to hardly feel anything due to the amount of adrenaline surging through their body.

This adrenaline will help you swim to shore. If you have a way of making yourself a tourniquet to stem the blood flow, so much the better. The two big dangers are loss of blood and dying of shock.

....

REMEMBER: *Most people survive shark attacks.*

....

'Clance,' Ruby said. 'Sharks are not interested in human flesh – most attacks happen by accident. The shark spots a swimmer, mistakes it for a seal and goes over to investigate. The problem comes because sharks explore with their teeth – more often than not they take a bite and think better of it.'

'That's very reassuring Rube – I feel a whole lot better – just wait while I go dive into the ocean.'

'What you gotta do,' continued Ruby, ignoring her friend's sarcasm, 'is try not to pee – they take this as a sign of vulnerability. Failing that, if he's got you in his jaws, bop him on the nose with your fist. The nose is very sensitive on a shark. He'll soon let go – on the whole sharks can't be bothered to fight. They're not used to it.'

'Well, there's a coincidence,' said Clancy, 'neither am I!'

....

FACT: You cannot outswim a shark.
FACT: A great white shark can detect a drop of blood in an Olympic-sized pool. In other words, these guys are excellent sniffers.

....

If you do get chomped a little then get yourself to shore as quickly as possible.

SNIFF...
SNIFF...
SNIFF...
IS THAT **PEE**?

It is very disconcerting to find yourself face to face with someone not of your species.

> *Ruby wasn't sure at first, but there was something strange about the way Mrs Hasselberg was drinking her coffee. Whenever she raised her cup to take a sip, she sort of dangled her finger in her drink, which seemed to cause an alarming gurgling sound. Ruby couldn't be a hundred per cent sure, but she suspected that Mrs Hasselberg might be drinking cappuccino through her index finger.*

What to do when confronted by alien life forms...

Firstly, you must ascertain if they are friend or foe. This can be difficult – remember they may not understand your customs or greetings. A smile and a handshake may be considered highly aggressive actions and mistaken for baring of teeth and grabbing of limb or, in some cases, tentacle.

Try to keep a respectful distance and not stare. If it transpires the alien in question is foe, act like you are unaware of their hostile status – i.e. just play along – and, when the moment allows, give them the slip and run like crazy.

WARNING: *ALIENS OFTEN HAVE CONCEALED ZAPPERS.*

OK, so not everyone believes in alien life forms and maybe you're one of them, but all I can say is it's best to observe **RULE 11** and **BE PREPARED**. The Boy Scouts have it right about that one.

Either way, if you believe or don't believe, the above can be very useful info for encounters with all kinds of folks from the murderous to the downright boring. (See 'Survival Etiquette', page 120.)

FRIEND OR FOE? *YOU DECIDE*

☞ RHINOS

Bad eyesight and great hearing make the rhino a little paranoid. Your best bet is to climb a tree if you're lucky enough to spot one while the rhino is charging. If you find yourself unable to get your jello legs climbing then stand behind the tree and cross your fingers.

All outta trees? Run in the opposite direction: rhinos are speedy on their feet (they can hit thirty-five miles an hour) but they are carrying a lot of weight so they aren't so quick at the turns.

☞ BEARS

The first thing you gotta know about bears is they are unpredictable. Sometimes the best thing you can do is drop to the ground and play dead and sometimes this action merely suggests an easy meal and can cause you to wind up mauled to death. Sometimes it's best to face up to them, making yourself as big as possible, and wave your arms and shout your head off, but oftentimes this just enrages them and you may end up *without a head*, you just never know. For this reason it's wise to avoid meeting a bear at all costs.

BAD IDEA #1

YOU ARE PROBABLY JUST ENRAGING THE ANIMAL.

How to avoid a bear...

Never carry food in your pockets, not a morsel, not a mint; bears have an exceptional sense of smell and they are scroungers. Always make a lot of noise when walking in bear country; bears hate to be surprised. If you spot a bear, try and get downwind of it so it can't sniff you out; these guys really have amazing noses.

✳ FACTS ABOUT BEARS

They can rip a car open like a tin can.

They smell very, very well. Some experts believe a bear can smell carrion (the flesh of a dead animal) from thirty kilometres away.

They can swim.

They can climb trees.

They can outrun a human, no problem at all.

They can dig.

They are stronger than the strongest man.

What to do if you should meet a bear...

Wish you hadn't.

BAD IDEA #2

CARRYING EVEN A MORSEL OF FOOD ON YOU, BOZO.

I have met some bears in my time, but all of them have been the human variety. Most people you can suss out, but some can be very unpredictable. Once you work out what makes 'em tick, you have the advantage, but until you do, never jump to any conclusions. You just have to go on instinct and your main instinct, like with bears, should be to get on outta there as fast as possible.

☛ TIGERS

Tigers are beautiful creatures as pretty much anyone will agree, but they are not to be messed with: they can break your neck as quick as look at you so it's important to avoid any kinda embrace with this particular big cat. If you should be so unfortunate as to come face to face with one, whatever you do:

WARNING: DON'T RUN.

Have you ever watched a house cat run after a mouse? You make a dash for it, you might as well grow a pair of big pink ears and a long tail because you're acting like said rodent.

This leaves your neck exposed and a tiger is looking to clamp its jaws round your neck and snap your spine. They can do this with one bite.

....

ADVICE: *Drop to the ground and play dead.*

....

This confuses them: they aren't expecting their prey to suddenly stop running – they don't know what it could mean. The thrill of the chase over, the tiger pads off – no guaranteed results, but it's your best chance and let's face it, chance is all you got.

Same goes for dealing with bullies and general taunting.

Ignoring them is often the best method – you give
nothing back, what's the joy in them bothering you?

'Hey, look who it is Gemma, little Red Ridingfort
and her helper, Nancy Drew.'

'Yeah,' sneered Gemma Melamare, applying
more make-up to her perfect, bland little face, 'do
you think they're off to goody-goody club?'

'I doubt it,' yawned Vapona, 'they are so
boring that even the squeaky cleans don't want
them hanging around.'

Ruby and Clancy sat down on the bench and,
milkshakes in hand, continued to talk.

Vapona and Gemma came right up close;
Vapona picked up Clancy's drink and sniffed it.

Ruby batted the air. 'I wouldn't touch that
Clance, there's some nasty bugs about.'

'Really?' said Clancy.

'Yeah, you can't be too careful,' said Ruby.

They carried on talking about other things
while Melamare and Bugwart did their best to
get up their noses. It was futile. Ruby and Clancy
were like Zen masters: Clancy had had years of
practice ignoring his sisters and Ruby, well, Ruby

had studied every book on the subject.

    'Can you hear a buzzing sound?' asked Clancy.

    'I can Clance, must be gnats or something. How about we split the scene?'

    'Yeah, good idea, I can smell a bad smell and I think it's attracting flies.'

On the other hand, you may want to do a Del Lasco[1] and sock 'em in the mouth. I am not suggesting this will work or that you should do it, but it's the only way Del Lasco knows: she is highly volatile when provoked.

WARNING: DON'T PROVOKE DEL LASCO.

9.

SURVIVAL ETIQUETTE

THERE ARE CERTAIN FORMAL OCCASIONS when a certain type of behaviour is required or indeed appreciated, occasions which involve etiquette. Etiquette basically means rules and rituals and customs. When to nod, bow, kneel, walk backwards – you get the idea.

☛ IF YOU SHOULD HAPPEN TO MEET THE QUEEN OF ENGLAND

Curtsey.

Or bow depending on your male/female status.

Call her Your Majesty.

After this first greeting is over, **you can call her mam as in ham not marm as in balm.**

i.e.:

Curtsey.

RUBY: 'Hello, Your Majesty.'

QoE: 'Hello and how are you?'

RUBY: 'Just swell mam.'

QoE: 'Oh, you're American.'

Queen extends hand; you shake it. Conversation over. You walk backwards three paces and curtsey or bow as applicable.

☛ MEETING THE AMBASSADOR

Call him or her *Your Excellency* – they like this as it makes them feel like being the ambassador was worth all the long hours and living in a rented home.

General note...

People who have titles – Lord, Lady, Viscount, Sir, Dame, etc. – really like you to use 'em so, if you want to get a titled person onside, don't forget to stick it on the envelope.

☞ DEALING WITH INDIVIDUALS WHO YOU SUSPECT MIGHT BE DANGEROUS

I have watched at least 500 TV shows where, during the episode, it dawns on one of the characters that the person they are in conversation with is, in fact, some kind of murdering psychopath.

Almost without fail, what they do next is to either... blurt out that they know:

FOOLISH SOON-TO-BE VICTIM: *'I thought it was you all along that murdered old Mr Caspian, but when I saw you loading that body bag into the trunk of your car, I knew for sure. No one else might have seen it, but I did. I'm gonna call the police right now and they'll be here in no time – so where's your phone?'*

EVIL PSYCHOPATH: **'Now what would I do with a phone? I don't have anyone to call... all dead, you see.'**

FOOLISH SOON-TO-BE VICTIM: *'OK, I guess I'll have to walk and, once I make it to the police station, I'm going to tell them just where you stowed the body.'*

EVIL PSYCHOPATH: **'And just how are you going to do that when you no longer have a head?'** {Evil laughter.}

Or they make their fear so obvious, via their body language, that the murdering psychopath is tipped off:

EVIL PSYCHOPATH: **'So, would you like to stay for a glass of lemonade or something?'**

FOOLISH SOON-TO-BE VICTIM: *'Yes, why not.'* {Spots large axe in corner of hallway, eyes drawn to drops of blood on stair carpet, gulps furtively, looks round room seeking escape route. Profuse sweating.} *'You know what, um, I suddenly feel a little queasy. I just might head off home.'* {Whites of eyes clearly visible.}

EVIL PSYCHOPATH: *'Head off you say...? Now that's an idea.'* {Evil laughter.}

Both these reactions lead to the individual becoming the next victim.

What you should do instead...

As in the alien example, act nice, keep friendly, make a plausible excuse and get out of there as quick as possible.

EVIL PSYCHOPATH: *'So, would you like to stay for a glass of lemonade or something?'*

YOU: *'Yes, that would be lovely, but could I trouble you to add some fresh mint in mine? Mint gives it that pizzazz, you know what I'm saying?'* {Casual delivery, easy-going shrug.}

EVIL PSYCHOPATH: *'I agree. I'll just get a sharp knife to cut it with.'*

YOU: *'I have a better idea: you get the ice from the icebox and I'll wander out into the garden and see if I can't find the mint. I'm so looking forward to that drink! Boy, am I ever in need of it!'* {Pocket the car keys unobserved, walk slowly out, smiling, taking in the day, whistle (hum if you can't whistle) – act your pants off. Get in that car and drive, bozo, drive!}

WARNING: *DON'T BE SURPRISED IF YOU FIND FRESH MINT LOSES ITS PIZZAZZ.*

☛ DEALING WITH INDIVIDUALS WHO YOU KNOW ARE DANGEROUSLY DULL

Here I am assuming that your aim is not to hurt the dull person's feelings.

In this situation you might want to fake a coughing fit: if they offer to assist by fetching you water, just wave weakly and indicate that you will do better if you sit alone in the bathroom until the fit passes. You can legitimately run from the scene without offending.

Sometimes one might be at a party or social gathering where drinks are served; here a popular ploy can be to offer to get your boring companion a beverage and then simply not return. This method leaves a lot to be desired since it is all too obvious what you are doing and feelings can be squashed.

Other ways out...

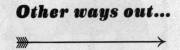

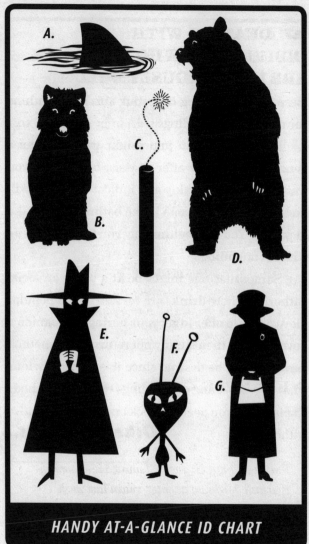

A: MAN-EATING SHARK B: CUNNING WOLF C: EXPLODING DYNAMITE D: VORACIOUS BEAR
E: EVIL PSYCHOPATH F: ALIEN FRIEND OR FOE G: HRH THE QUEEN OF ENGLAND

HANDY AT-A-GLANCE ID CHART

✳ EXAMPLE 1

Fake sudden memory of an appointment you are meant to be at or a phone call you urgently need to make. You can cleverly link this to something your boring companion is droning on about; this leads them to believe that your vacating the area is spontaneous.

> **BORING INDIVIDUAL:** *'In 1972 I had a wonderful summer break watching antelope bathe in a watering hole.'*

> **YOU:** *'Oh my good gosh! That reminds me, I'm meant to be meeting Aunty Lopes at the swimming baths! Excuse me while I skedaddle.'*

✳ EXAMPLE 2

Explain that you need to check on an ageing relative without delay.

> *'I must call my Grandpa Louie. He's seventy-two and fell down a water main last week while on vacation.'*

✳ EXAMPLE 3

Introduce your companion to another party-goer, continue conversing for three minutes and give them both the slip.

> *'Clancy, you must meet Alice Meindnumb! We've been having the most fascinating conversation about antelope bathing... talking of which I might just take a little trip to the bathroom myself.'* {Scowl from Clancy.}

✳ EXAMPLE 4

Excuse yourself to help the host.

> *'Sounds like our host is trying to wrestle a whole herd of antelope in the kitchen. I'll just see what I can do to help.'*

✳ EXAMPLE 5

Start acting strangely.

> *'Antelopes! That takes me back to my student days. I once lived with one you know, very personable, but after a while his knees gave up; he was afraid of the elevator you see and living in an apartment block with nineteen flights of stairs did him no good at all, especially on the days when he went grocery shopping.'*

Boring individual will excuse himself and rush from scene.

BEWARE THIS SITUATION

When nothing else comes to mind...

Faint.

* * *

9 ½.

WHEN ETIQUETTE FAILS: GET ME OUTTA HERE SIGNALS

SOMETIMES WORDS WILL FAIL YOU, other times the obvious words can be too obvious, and sometimes words are just not an option – this is when *get me outta here* signals can come in handy.

☞ FIRE

Looking to be spotted by a plane or ship? OK, buster: light three fires. This is an internationally recognised distress signal.

☞ MORSE CODE

Morse code is pretty useful. Me and Clancy Crew use it all the time to communicate in class. But if you're not gonna learn the whole alphabet, you need to at least remember one little word: **SOS**.

This is maybe the most famous signal in the world and you can make it with a torch, a fire, a radio – all sorts of things.

Here's what you need to know buster:

LETTER	IN MORSE CODE	OR...
S	*dot dot dot*	**...**
O	*dash dash dash*	**– – –**
SOS	*dot dot dot dash dash dash dot dot dot*	**...– – –...**

Imagine you're in a life raft at night and you see a ship passing. You have a torch in your kit. What you do is use the on/off switch to make:

✳✳✳ *Three short flashes.*

✳✳✳ Three long flashes.

✳✳✳ *Then three short flashes again.*

So, you just signalled SOS in Morse code and now you gotta sit on that raft and hope like crazy that that big old ship makes an about-turn and picks you up. You gotta cross your fingers that the captain wasn't taking a little bathroom break when you were signalling your distress. If he was, you better take a look at the 'Marooned at sea' section on page 67.

☛ AN ESCAPE WORD

This can be a very good idea when you are in a tight spot: bored to tears at a social engagement, needing to get outta somewhere fast, trying to communicate that you have been captured by a dangerous criminal without letting on you are actually asking to be rescued. These are all good

reasons to use an escape word.

> *Clancy Crew tried to remember all the*
> *things Ruby had said during their telephone*
> *conversation just the other night. That had been*
> *the last time Clancy had heard from Ruby. Had*
> *Ruby been trying to tell him something? Maybe*
> *she had been captured by some arch-villain and*
> *was trying to let Clancy know her whereabouts in*
> *some sort of code.*
>
> *Now Clancy thought of it, it did seem strange*
> *that Ruby had mentioned that she was having*
> *tapioca pudding in China. Ruby Redfort hated*
> *tapioca pudding – everybody knew that! And just*
> *what was she doing in China?*

Don't pick a word that is either too common or too obscure. For example: **cat**.

It would be awkward if the subject of cats came up in conversation if this was your escape code word.

Equally, don't get too complicated. For example: you might find it a bit of a struggle and therefore a giveaway trying to work **xylophone** into your conversation.

VILLAIN: *'Would you like to stay for dinner in my remote castle?'*

YOU: *'Well, the thing is, I ought to go home and practise my xylophone.'*

✳ A GOOD ESCAPE WORD EXAMPLE

Canary is a good code word because it isn't commonly used in chit-chat, but can be inserted easily into most conversations.

BOTHERSOME PERSON: *'Can I show you my collection of unusual hats? The unusual thing about them is that they are all exactly the same.'*

YOU: *'I bought a wonderful canary yellow hat last week that would be divine with those pants.'* {Means: Let's split the scene before my brain stops functioning.}

Or maybe:

YOU: *'Have you ever been to the Canary Islands? They have wonderful hats there.'* {Means: Boy, is this guy ever the biggest yawn yet? Let's beat it my friend before we lose the will to live.}

Or just:

....

YOU: *'I'm telling you, when I found these shoes marked down to half price, I must have looked like the cat that got the canary.'*
{Means: If you don't get me outta here quick, I'm gonna turn into this guy.}

Or even:

....

CREEPY VILLAIN: *'So, would you like to stay for dinner at my remote castle? I'm sure I can find a bite... or two... to eat.'* **Shifty look.**

YOU: *'You're too kind! Here I am chirping on like a canary when you're obviously hungry and looking for nice warm prey, I mean praying for a nice warm meal. No, we'll just get out of your lair... I mean hair... and leave you to it. We'll catch up some other time.'*
{Means: This guy is gonna kill us for sure – he's obviously some kinda vampire. Let's beat it before he tucks in.}

10.

CONCLUSION: NOW YOU KNOW WHAT TO DO WHEN YOUR WORST WORRY COMES YOUR WAY

You've nearly made it, bozo...

☞ SO, THE BASIC RULES OF SURVIVAL ARE AS FOLLOWS:

Keep a cool head – don't panic.

If you're with others then work as a team.

Find shelter, warmth and water.

Think sideways – the obvious solution is not always the best.

Improvise – don't be defeated.

And above all tell yourself you're gonna make it out of there no matter what.

OK, so this isn't everything, not by a long shot, but it might be enough to make you see that a lot of survival is all about attitude and if you know that then it might encourage you to get some.

So, you're walking along one day sniffing roses when all of a sudden a rhino charges, but you give him the slip by turning suddenly, he's wrong footed, you run in the opposite direction only to find yourself falling through air, you reach out and now you're clinging onto a cliff edge by the fingernails and feeling a tad thirsty...

What do you do?

....

REMEMBER: **NEVER SAY DIE.**

....

⟫⟫→ STOP.

⟫⟫→ THINK.

⟫⟫→ DECIDE TO BE CALM.

⟫⟫→ FOCUS ON THAT GLASS OF ICE-COLD LEMONADE.

And hang on in there, bozo...

LAUREN CHILD first introduced the character of Ruby Redfort in her three award-winning, bestselling CLARICE BEAN novels (*Utterly Me, Clarice Bean; Clarice Bean Spells Trouble* and *Clarice Bean, Don't Look Now*). Since then she has been inundated with letters from fans asking for the RUBY REDFORT books. And it must have worked, because two books – *Ruby Redfort: Look Into My Eyes* and *Ruby Redfort: Take Your Last Breath* – have already been published. Not to mention the handy pocket-sized survival guide you are currently holding in your hands!

Lauren is also the creator of the phenomenally successful CHARLIE AND LOLA books, as well as Associate Producer on the TV show of the same name. She has sold millions of books around the world and won many prizes, including the Smarties Prize (four times), the Kate Greenaway Medal and the Red House Children's Book Award.

To sign up for the Ruby Redfort newsletter and for puzzles, codes, videos, games and more, head to

www.rubyredfort.com

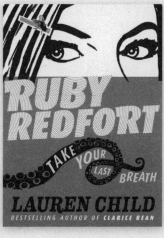